Issues in Action

IMMIGRATION, REFUGEES, AND THE FIGHT FOR A BETTER LIFE

Elliott Smith

Cicely Lewis, Executive Editor

Lerner Publications ◆ Minneapolis

LETTER FROM CICELY LEWIS

Dear Reader,

I started the Read Woke challenge in response to the needs of my students. I wanted my students to read books that challenged social norms, gave voice to the voiceless, and sought to challenge the status quo. Have you ever felt as if the truth was being hidden from you? Have

Cicely Lewis

you ever felt like adults are not telling you the full story because you are too young? Well, I believe you have a right to know about the issues that are plaguing our society. I believe that you have a right to hear the truth.

I created Read Woke Books because I want you to be knowledgeable and compassionate citizens. You will be the leaders of our society soon, and you need to be equipped with knowledge so that you can treat others with the dignity and respect they deserve. And so you can be treated with that same respect.

As you turn these pages, learn about how history has impacted the things we do today. Hopefully you can be the change that helps to make our world a better place for all.

—Cicely Lewis, Executive Editor

TABLE OF CONTENTS

A section of fence along the border between Mexico and the United States

NO PLACE TO GO

ON THE BORDER BETWEEN MEXICO AND THE UNITED STATES, THOUSANDS OF IMMIGRANTS ARE HELD AGAINST THEIR WILL IN GUARDED FACILITIES. They crossed the border into the US, most in an attempt to make a better life. But current US law makes crossing the border a criminal offense. Strict laws and enforcement mean that agencies such as Customs and Border Control and Immigration and Customs Enforcement (ICE) have the authority to lock immigrants away, sometimes for months, as they wait for court proceedings. Beginning in 2018, many families were split up and children were separated from their parents.

No one knows exactly how many people are held at these detention centers on a given day. But one government count estimated that by January 2020, more than forty-three hundred children had been separated from their parents. Many report poor conditions at the overcrowded facilities. Journalists discovered children sleeping on concrete floors, a lack of hygiene products such as soap and toothpaste, and exposure to diseases including chicken pox.

The anger around conditions at the border and the laws that enabled them have led to protests across the country. In June 2018, as news of family separations came to light, marchers hit the streets in Washington, DC, and elsewhere to protest.

Protesters hold signs criticizing deportations and ICE.

Reports of unsafe facilities also drew the attention of elected officials, some of whom traveled to tour them.

"This has been horrifying so far," US representative Alexandria Ocasio-Cortez wrote after her visit. "It is hard to [overstate] the enormity of the problem."

Many individuals and organizations are committed to changing both the laws and the attitudes about immigration in the US. They fight for the human rights of immigrants who are detained and hope to prevent abuses in the future.

Representative Alexandria Ocasio-Cortez speaks to a migrant mother whose daughter died in ICE custody in 2019.

A boat carries immigrants to Ellis Island around 1910.

CHAPTER 1
A LAND OF DREAMS

FOR ALL OF HUMAN HISTORY, PEOPLE HAVE MOVED FROM ONE PLACE TO ANOTHER TO FIND RESOURCES, ESCAPE CONFLICT, AND EXPLORE. Over time, different regions of the world rose and fell in wealth and influence, and people moved around accordingly.

Those who move to new countries are categorized as either immigrants or refugees. Immigrants choose to move to another country. In many cases, moving is an attempt to create a better life. Most countries have a legal process that immigrants must follow to gain citizenship. But many immigrants remain undocumented, meaning they lack the legal paperwork to become citizens of a country. National governments may deport these people, or force them to leave.

Refugees are forced to move because they fear harm. Refugees often face danger because of religious or political beliefs. Many simply wish to escape from homelands with high crime rates or oppressive governments. Refugees may apply for asylum in their new country. Asylum means that a government will protect those fleeing danger at home. But obtaining asylum is a complex legal process. And it can be difficult for people to prove they are fleeing real danger.

Immigrants wait in line to enter the US through Ellis Island. Many underwent legal and medical inspections.

Between 1850 and 1882, San Francisco, California, was a main port of entry for immigrants from China to the US.

The US has a long history of immigration. Many come in search of the American Dream, the idea that anyone can succeed with enough hard work. During a forty-year period starting in 1880, more than twenty million immigrants arrived in the US, most from Europe. Many immigrants from around the world started businesses, built or bought homes, and raised families. The US has also resettled thousands of refugees. Between 1980 and 2000, the US resettled over fifty thousand refugees per year.

But newcomers often face a difficult reality. Low wages, poor living conditions, racism, and language barriers can make life challenging. And the US government has often been hostile to immigrants. Some laws, such as the Chinese Exclusion Act of 1882, restricted or denied access to certain groups of people, often on the basis of racism or fear of foreigners. Other laws, such as the 1996 Illegal Immigration Reform and Immigrant Responsibility Act (IIRAIRA), made it easier for the government to deport people and harder for immigrants to obtain legal status. At different points in history, the US has placed quotas on who is allowed in the country and created harsh penalties for undocumented immigrants.

"As an immigrant, you work three times as hard and are promised maybe a fraction as much."

—Lin-Manuel Miranda, creator of *Hamilton*

Still, the hope of a better life is hard to resist. More than one million immigrants arrive in the US each year.

Customs and Border Patrol officers take someone's application for a special security pass. Certain passes allow people to pass quickly between the US and Mexico.

CHAPTER 2
A NATIONAL ISSUE

UP TO TWELVE MILLION UNDOCUMENTED IMMIGRANTS LIVE IN THE US. For years, legislators have disagreed about how to create immigration laws that treat people fairly and provide legal options for those who want to enter the country. And many are opposed to allowing more people to enter the US. In 2016 Donald Trump was elected president after making immigration limitations a key part of his campaign.

Both legal and illegal immigration are difficult processes. Racism often influences who gains citizenship or asylum. In the nineteenth and twentieth centuries, laws required that immigrants pass health or literacy tests to enter the country.

These tests provided a way to discriminate against certain immigrants without specifically naming race or ethnicity. One test, for example, required that immigrants read and write a passage from the US Constitution upon arriving in the country.

IIRAIRA greatly increased deportations in the US in the 1990s. In 2016 more than 340,000 people were removed from the country, over five times more than in 1995. By 2020 agencies such as ICE had gained sweeping power to detain and deport undocumented immigrants, even those who had lived in the US for years.

REFLECT

How do you think the media reinforces stereotypes of immigrants, and how might those stereotypes lead to prejudice?

ICE was formed in 2003 as a part of the Department of Homeland Security. The department was created in response to the terrorist attacks on September 11, 2001.

Donald Trump speaks at a campaign rally in October 2016. Trump often used rallies to speak against illegal immigration.

As president, Trump worked to enact his agenda to limit immigration. He tried several times to overturn Deferred Action for Childhood Arrivals (DACA). Passed in 2012, DACA gave work permits and deportation deferrals to undocumented immigrants who came to the US as children and had no criminal records. Trump also adopted a zero-tolerance policy that treated both undocumented immigrants and asylum seekers at the US-Mexico border as criminals. Overworked immigration courts, crowded facilities, and confused legal processes all contributed to the crisis there.

Statistics show that immigrants contribute greatly to the US economy. Immigrants make up 17 percent of the

Out of between two and three million farmworkers in the US, about three-fourths are immigrants. Half of those are undocumented.

workforce, with undocumented immigrants a significant portion of that number. Immigrants will also play a major role in US population growth going forward. When polled, most Americans are in favor of immigration. Seventy-six percent describe it as "a good thing for the country."

> "At one point, our country, our constitution, and our democracy did not recognize women, did not recognize Black people . . . we have been [on] this journey as a country to really live up to the best of the ideals that founded this country: of justice, of equality for everyone."
>
> —Cristina Jiménez, cofounder of United We Dream, a youth-led immigrant organization

A Syrian refugee family at a camp in Passau, Germany, in 2015

CHAPTER 3
A GLOBAL CRISIS

IMMIGRATION ISSUES DON'T BELONG ONLY TO THE US. In the twenty-first century, people all over the world leave their homes for a variety of reasons. They flee war, famine, racism, religious discrimination, and natural disasters. According to the United Nations, nearly twenty-six million people were refugees in 2020. Almost half of them are under the age of eighteen.

In the search for new homes, some refugees are met with hostility. Increased border security, military actions, and even jail time are among the measures nations take to keep refugees out. Some countries claim they do not have the resources to house and feed refugees. Temporary camps

Palestinian refugees pick up food supplies at a distribution center run by the United Nations.

and settlements can be dangerous for those on the move. Many refugees do not have basic human rights or any sort of political voice to improve their situation.

In the 2010s, refugee departure hot spots included Syria, Afghanistan, South Sudan, and Myanmar. Beginning in 2014, thousands fled instability, violence, and lack of access to essential services in Venezuela. By the end of 2019, more than four million had fled. More than one hundred thousand Venezuelans had applied for asylum in the US as of March 2020.

AT GREATER RISK

During times of crisis, women often face a greater risk of unequal or even harmful treatment. As refugees, women are often subjected to violent physical attacks. In shelters and refugee camps, they may be denied medical care or hygiene products. Activists urge humanitarian organizations to take steps to ensure that women are protected on the road to safety.

A woman cooks at a refugee camp in Dunkirk, France.

Migrant children stand outside a detention center in Homestead, Florida. The for-profit center was shut down in November 2019 amid charges of child neglect and abuse.

Many Central Americans have fled drug-related gang wars in countries such as El Salvador, Guatemala, and Honduras. But general violence in an area is not legally considered a reason for asylum, leaving these families without legal status.

Organizations around the world are dedicated to helping refugees resettle in new countries. Turkey is one of the most popular relocation spots for refugees. In 2020 it hosted more than 3.5 million refugees. In the US, the complex vetting process for refugees can take as long as two years. Between 2016 and 2020, the number of refugees resettled yearly in the US dropped from nearly 85,000 to about 11,000.

The Families Belong Together rally protested the Trump administration's family separation policy in June 2018.

CHAPTER 4
A BETTER TOMORROW

WHEN DAVID XOL AND HIS SEVEN-YEAR-OLD SON BYRON LEFT THEIR NATIVE GUATEMALA FOR THE US IN 2018, THEY EMBARKED ON A DIFFICULT JOURNEY. It ended with their capture by US authorities at the border. Due to zero-tolerance policies, Xol was sent back to Guatemala. Byron remained in a detention facility in the US with other separated kids.

In January 2020 a federal judge ruled that the US government had wrongfully prevented some parents and children from seeking asylum. At the Los Angeles airport, happy reunions took place for nine families who had been separated from their children. Xol was able to tearfully hug Byron, who had since turned nine. "He grew a lot," Xol said of his son.

While the Xols were able to celebrate, thousands of children have yet to reunite with their parents. In October 2020 reports found that the parents of 545 children could not be located, meaning the families may be permanently separated. The fight for immigrants' human rights continues. Many organizations are dedicated to ensuring immigrant children see their families again.

The Xols' reunion at the Los Angeles International Airport in January 2020

TOGETHER FOR JUSTICE

The immigrant rights movement overlaps in many ways with the fight for racial justice. During the civil rights movement of the 1950s and 1960s, many Black activists found common ground with immigrants fighting for equality. In the decades since, many members of these groups have joined forces in a larger social justice movement, working toward connected causes and calling for change.

Marchers protest segregated schools in Trenton, New Jersey, in 1963.

Many immigrants find happy homes in their new countries.

Human Rights Watch, the American Civil Liberties Union (ACLU), and United We Dream are just some of the groups dedicated to speaking out and helping immigrants. They provide free legal services, educate communities, lobby governments, and organize media coverage around their missions. They work in hopes that someday all immigrants and refugees will be able to live safe, happy lives.

REFLECT

How could countries work together to create a network of safe places for refugees?

Perhaps the best advocates for immigrant rights are immigrants themselves. The young adults protected by DACA are known as Dreamers. Many Dreamers became activists, speaking out for their rights and the rights of other immigrants.

"We all have different backgrounds, first and last names, interests, journeys, and goals," said DACA recipient Alonso R. Reyna Rivarola. "However, we all have at least one thing in common: we are all American Dreamers."

An activist speaks at an event protesting the Trump administration's move to end DACA in 2017.

TAKE ACTION

Here are some ways you and your family can help support immigrants and refugees:

Write or call your local, state, and national representatives and express your concerns.

Support migrant families in your neighborhood. Make friends at school with kids who may be new to the country.

With an adult's help, aid families recently released from detention by donating to organizations that provide necessary materials.

Find out more from organizations that deal with immigration and refugee issues.

Amnesty USA: https://www.amnestyusa.org/our-work

United Nations Refugee Agency: https://www.unhcr.org/en-us

United We Dream: https://unitedwedream.org/about/#mission

TIMELINE

1790: Congress passes the US's first immigration law. Free white people may apply for citizenship.

1820: The first wave of European immigrants arrives in the US from Ireland and Germany.

1882: The Chinese Exclusion Act bars Chinese immigrants from entering the US.

1892: The Ellis Island immigrant inspection station opens in New York Harbor. More than twelve million immigrants would enter the US here before its closure in 1954.

1924: The Immigration Act places quotas on who can enter the US. The act favors immigrants from northern and western Europe and bars most immigration from Asia and Africa.

1952: The Immigration and Nationality Act formally ends the exclusion of Asian immigrants.

1965: The new Immigration and Nationality Act ends the immigration quota system.

1986: President Ronald Reagan signs a bill pardoning three million undocumented immigrants.

1996: President Bill Clinton signs IIRAIRA, which increases penalties for undocumented immigrants who violate US law, among other changes. Deportations skyrocket.

2012: President Obama signs DACA, an executive order protecting undocumented youth from deportation.

2018: President Trump announces a zero-tolerance policy that separates families attempting to enter the US illegally.

GLOSSARY

advocate: someone who speaks up for or helps a person or cause, or the act of doing so

asylum: protection given by a government to someone who has left another country

deport: to force a person who is not a citizen to leave a country

discriminate: to treat in a biased or unfair way

famine: a mass food shortage

literacy: the ability to read and write

quota: an official limit on how many people or things are allowed

undocumented: lacking the documents required for citizenship or residency

SOURCE NOTES

6   Alison Durkee, "AOC Goes to the Border, Shares the 'Systemic Cruelty' of the Migrant Detention Centers," *Vanity Fair*, July 2, 2019, https://www.vanityfair.com/news/2019/07/aoc-ocasio -cortez-congress-migrant-detention-centers.

10 Oprah Winfrey, "Oprah Talks to Lin-Manuel Miranda about Immigrant Grit," *O, The Oprah Magazine*, July 6, 2018, https:// www.oprahmag.com/entertainment/a22593426/oprah-lin -manuel-miranda-interview-puerto-rico.

14 Jeffrey M. Jones, "New High in U.S. Say Immigration Most Important Problem," Gallup, June 21, 2019, https://news.gallup .com/poll/259103/new-high-say-immigration-important -problem.aspx.

14 Nicole Carroll, "Cristina Jiménez Moreta Helped Get DACA, Now She Helps Young Immigrants Find Their Voice," *USA Today*, August 27, 2020, https://www.usatoday.com/in-depth /life/women-of-the-century/2020/08/20/cristina-jimenez -moreta-advocates-daca-undocumented-youth-human -rights/5535786002.

20 Nomaan Merchant and Elliot Spagat, "9 Parents Separated from Families Return to Children in the US," ABC News, January 23, 2020, https://abcnews.go.com/Politics/wireStory/migrant -parents-separated-kids-2018-return-us-68472318.

23 Alonso R. Reyna Rivarola, "American Dreamers," *New York Times*, accessed December 18, 2020, https://www.nytimes .com/interactive/projects/storywall/american-dreamers /stories/alonsor-reyna-rivarola.

READ WOKE READING LIST

Adewumi, Tanitoluwa. *My Name Is Tani . . . and I Believe in Miracles.* Nashville: Thomas Nelson, 2020.

Britannica Kids: Immigration
https://kids.britannica.com/kids/article/immigration/399508

Britannica Kids: Refugees
https://kids.britannica.com/kids/article/refugee/390620

Guerrero, Diane, and Erica Moroz. *My Family Divided: One Girl's Journey of Home, Loss, and Hope.* New York: Henry Holt, 2018.

Kids Discover: Immigration
https://www.kidsdiscover.com/shop/issues/immigration
-for-kids

Krull, Kathleen. *American Immigration: Our History, Our Stories.* New York: HarperCollins, 2020.

National Geographic Kids: Countries
https://kids.nationalgeographic.com/explore/countries

Shmuel, Naomi. *Too Far from Home.* Minneapolis: Kar-Ben Publishing, 2020.

INDEX

PHOTO ACKNOWLEDGMENTS

Image credits: Chess Ocampo/Shutterstock.com, p. 4; AP Photo/Mary Altaffer, p. 5; AP Photo/Tom Williams/CQ Roll Call, p. 6; Bain News Service via Library of Congress, p. 7; Everett Collection/Shutterstock.com, p. 8; CPA Media Pte Ltd/Alamy Stock Photo, p. 9; Rebekah Zemansky/Shutterstock.com, p. 11; © U.S. Immigration and Customs Enforcement, p. 12; Matt Smith Photographer/Shutterstock.com, p. 13; Andy Alfaro/The Modesto Bee/TNS/Alamy Live News, p. 14; Jazzmany/Shutterstock.com, p. 15; AP Photo/Hatem Moussa, p. 16; Anjo Kan/Shutterstock.com, p. 17; Storms Media Group/Alamy Stock Photo, p. 18; Rena Schild/Shutterstock.com, p. 19; AP Photo/Ringo H.W. Chiu, p. 20; AP Photo, p. 21; Zurijeta/Shutterstock.com, p. 22; Diego G Diaz/Shutterstock.com, p. 23. Cecily Lewis portrait photos by Fernando Decillis.

Design elements: Reddavebatcave/Shutterstock.com; Alexey Pushkin/Shutterstock.com; Alisara Zilch/Shutterstock.com.

Content consultant: Deepinder Singh Mayell, Executive Director and Lecturer in Law, James H. Binger Center for New Americans at the University of Minnesota Law School

Lerner Publications Company
An imprint of Lerner Publishing Group, Inc.
241 First Avenue North
Minneapolis, MN 55401 USA

For reading levels and more information, look up this title at www.lernerbooks.com.

Main body text set in Aptifer Sans LT Pro.
Typeface provided by Linotype AG.

Designer: Viet Chu **Photo Editor:** Sarah Kallemeyn
Lerner team: Martha Kranes

Library of Congress Cataloging-in-Publication Data

Names: Smith, Elliott, 1976– author.
Title: Immigration, refugees, and the fight for a better life / Elliott Smith.
Description: Minneapolis : Lerner Publications, [2022] | Series: Issues in action (Read Woke Books) | Includes bibliographical references and index. | Audience: Ages 9–14 | Audience: Grades 4–6 | Summary: "Readers look at the issue of immigration in the US and globally, examining the history, laws, and causes surrounding immigrants' and refugees' search for a better life and the difficulties they face"— Provided by publisher.
Identifiers: LCCN 2020040851 (print) | LCCN 2020040852 (ebook) | ISBN 9781728423418 (library binding) | ISBN 9781728430676 (ebook)
Subjects: LCSH: Emigration and immigration—Juvenile literature. | United States—Emigration and immigration—Juvenile literature. | Immigrants—Juvenile literature. | Refugees—Juvenile literature.
Classification: LCC JV6035 .S535 2022 (print) | LCC JV6035 (ebook) | DDC 325.73—dc23

LC record available at https://lccn.loc.gov/2020040851
LC ebook record available at https://lccn.loc.gov/2020040852

Manufactured in the United States of America
1-49179-49310-2/15/2021